BABY ANIMAL ZOO

Look for these
books in
The Kids in Ms. Colman's Class series

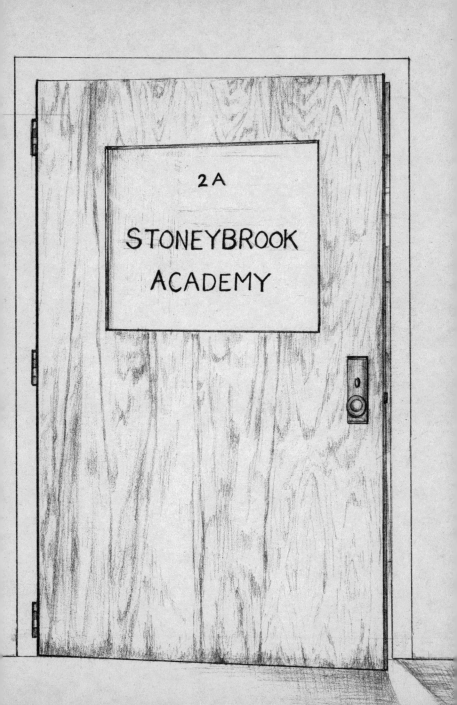

Jannie, Bobby, Tammy, Sara
Ian, Leslie, Hank, Terri, Pamela
Nancy, Omar, Audrey, Chris, Ms. Colman
Karen, Hannie, Ricky, Natalie

THE KIDS IN MS. COLMAN'S CLASS

BABY ANIMAL ZOO

Ann M. Martin

Illustrations by Charles Tang

A
LITTLE APPLE
PAPERBACK

SCHOLASTIC INC.
New York Toronto London Auckland Sydney

*The author gratefully acknowledges
Gabrielle Charbonnet
for her help
with this book.*

No part of this publication may be reproduced in whole or in part, or stored
in a retrieval system, or transmitted in any form or by any means, electronic,
mechanical, photocopying, recording, or otherwise, without written permission of the publisher. For information regarding permission, write to
Scholastic Inc., Attention: Permissions Department, 555 Broadway, New
York, NY 10012.

ISBN 0-590-06009-0

12 11 10 9 8 7 6 5 4 3 2 1   8 9/9 0 1 2 3/0

Printed in the U.S.A.   40
First Scholastic printing, March 1998

HOPSCOTCH

"**W**ant to play hopscotch?" Jannie Gilbert asked Pamela Harding.

Pamela thought hopscotch was a baby game. But it *was* sort of fun. And she was good at it. Pamela had often seen older girls playing it — even girls in fourth and fifth grade. She guessed they did not think it was babyish.

"Okay," Pamela said. Jannie, Pamela, and Leslie Morris ran to one of the hopscotch games that no one was using. Jannie and Leslie were Pamela's two best friends at Stoneybrook Academy in Stoneybrook, Connecticut. They were all in Class 2A, Ms. Colman's second grade. Pamela had been in Ms. Colman's class for a couple of months. Jannie and Leslie had known each other (and practically everyone else in Ms. Colman's class) since kindergarten.

At the hopscotch game, Pamela took off her necklace. It was a silver chain with a silver heart charm on it. She held it up.

"This is my marker," she said. Everyone knew that chains made the best markers because they almost always landed where you threw them. They did not roll or slide very much.

"I have my lucky key chain," said Jannie, pulling it out.

Leslie frowned. "I will have to use a rock." She looked on the ground by the fence for a rock. It could not be too round or too flat. It could not be too small or too big.

"Come on, Leslie," called Pamela. "We will be here all day!" Pamela tapped her foot and rolled her eyes. "Just grab a rock and let's go!"

"Yeah, Leslie," said Jannie. "Let's go!"

Leslie grabbed a rock and ran back to the game. She put her marker on the first square, next to Pamela's necklace and Jannie's key chain.

"Finally," said Pamela. "Let's do one-potato, two-potato to see who goes first."

"Okay," said Jannie.

"Okay," said Leslie.

Pamela was not surprised that they agreed with her. Jannie and Leslie almost always agreed with Pamela. That was why they were her best friends.

When Pamela and her family had moved to Stoneybrook, she had left all her old friends behind. Friends she had had since kindergarten. It had been so, so hard. When she had first come to Ms. Colman's class, she had not known how to make new friends. But after the first week or two, Jannie and Leslie had started hanging out with her. That was fine with Pamela. At least Jannie and Leslie were not goody-goody babies, like some of the other girls in Ms. Colman's class. And they were not loudmouthed know-it-alls, like one girl in particular.

When Pamela was on ninesies, Tammy and Terri Barkan came over to the game. Terri and Tammy were twins. They were in Ms. Colman's class too. Counting Pamela, there were eleven girls in Ms. Colman's class and only six boys.

"Are you going to be much longer?" asked Terri. "We want to play a game with Natalie and Sara. And school is about to start."

"Um," said Leslie.

"Too bad," Pamela said. She had to let the Barkan twins know who was boss. She carefully hopped back, picking up her necklace on the way. Then she threw her marker down to number ten. It landed exactly in the middle, without touching a single line. "We are going to play all the way back too."

"No fair," said Tammy. "Your game should be over when you finish tensies."

"Not this time," said Pamela. She

hopped right over the ten and off the hop-scotch game. Then she leaned over and picked up her marker again.

Tammy and Terri walked away, frowning at her. They put their heads together and talked angrily. Pamela did not hear what they were saying. And she did not care.

"Those babies," she said. And she began hopping again.

2
Ms. Colman's Class

When the bell rang, Pamela and Jannie picked up their hopscotch markers. (Leslie did not have to save her rock.) Then they walked slowly to Ms. Colman's class. Pamela always walked slowly when the bell rang. Running to class was babyish.

And since Pamela walked slowly, so did Leslie and Jannie.

Inside Ms. Colman's room, Pamela strolled to her desk. Jannie and Leslie went to theirs. Leslie sat next to Pamela, but Jannie sat one row back and one chair over.

All around her, Pamela's classmates

were running to their desks, talking and laughing. Chris Lamar was feeding Hootie, the class guinea pig. Karen Brewer, Hannie Papadakis, and Nancy Dawes were still talking. They called themselves the Three Musketeers.

Karen was Pamela's best enemy. She was a loudmouth. She could not sit still. And she hardly ever remembered to raise her hand in class before she spoke.

Ms. Colman walked into their room. "Good morning, class," she said with a smile. "Please take your seats."

Pamela sat up a little straighter. She liked Ms. Colman. Ms. Colman did not play favorites. And she could make almost anything sound interesting.

"Omar, could you please take attendance for me?" asked Ms. Colman.

Omar Harris walked to the front of the room. He opened the attendance book and got his pen ready.

"Tammy and Terri Barkan?" Omar began. "Karen Brewer? Nancy Dawes? Sara

Ford? Bobby Gianelli? Jannie Gilbert? Audrey Green? Pamela Harding? Me — I am here. Ian Johnson? Chris Lamar? Leslie Morris? Hannie Papadakis? Hank Reubens? Natalie Springer? Ricky Torres? Everyone is here, Ms. Colman."

"Thank you, Omar," she said. "Now, class, I have an announcement to make."

"Oh, goody!" said Karen. "Goody gumdrops."

There she goes again, thought Pamela. Shouting out without raising her hand.

"Remember our unit on wild animals?" asked Ms. Colman. "Today we are going to start another unit on animals. But this time we will learn about baby animals."

Leslie looked at Pamela and smiled. Pamela did not smile back.

"Please open your science books to page sixty-three," said Ms. Colman. "It is a chapter about animal parents and their young. Does anyone know what a baby goat is called?"

"A kid!" said Bobby.

"What about a baby pig?" asked Ms. Colman.

"A piglet," said Hannie. "Everyone knows that."

"And a horse?"

"A colt," said Karen.

"A colt is a baby male horse," explained Ms. Colman. "A baby female horse is called a filly. A foal is a baby horse of either sex."

Pamela yawned behind her hand. Ani-

mals did not interest her very much. Why did they have to do a whole unit on them?

"Audrey, could you please begin reading the chapter?" asked Ms. Colman.

"Animals everywhere have babies," Audrey read. "Some have live babies. Some lay eggs. In this chapter, we will see how different kinds of animals reproduce. First we will look at reptiles."

"Thank you, Audrey," said Ms. Colman. "Karen, could you read the next paragraph?"

Karen began to read. Pamela looked at Leslie and rolled her eyes. Then she propped her chin on her hand and looked down at her science book. Why couldn't they learn about something else, like weather? Pamela liked weather. There were many different kinds of weather. Some kinds of weather were very exciting, such as tornadoes and hurricanes.

Pamela sighed and turned the page in her science book. Tornadoes would be much better to learn about than baby reptiles.

ON THE PLAYGROUND

"I think spring is on the way," said Jannie the next day. "It is much warmer." She, Pamela, and Leslie were in line to play foursquare at recess.

"I will be glad not to have to wear a coat anymore," said Pamela. "I hate being all bundled up."

"Me too," said Leslie. "Hats and mittens and gloves and scarves. Winter is a pain."

"You are right," said Pamela. "I like springtime, with flowers and new grass and no snow."

"Me too," said Jannie.

The three of them played foursquare

13

for awhile. Pamela liked foursquare. It was not babyish. It was hard to play well. It was fast and exciting. She stayed in the first box for a long time. Finally she got hit out by Hank Reubens. Pamela, Leslie, and Jannie walked around the playground.

"Hey, Natalie," said Pamela. "Did you tape your socks up today?"

"Oh, be quiet," said Natalie. She headed off to play jump rope with Tammy, Audrey, and Sara.

Pamela giggled. Natalie's socks were always falling down. She was famous for it. Pamela liked to tease her about different ways to make her socks stay up. Leslie and Jannie giggled too.

Karen, Hannie, and Nancy were playing under the big oak tree in the yard. They had made little piles of acorns. Pamela did not know what they were doing.

"It's the Three *Weird*keteers," said Pamela.

"Who asked you?" retorted Hannie.

Pamela grinned and kept walking.

In one corner of the playground was a jungle gym. Bobby had climbed to the very top of it, high in the air.

"Come on, you guys," he called down to Chris and Omar. They stood at the bottom of the jungle gym, looking up at him. "Come up here. I am at the top of a pirate ship, looking for land. You can help me look."

"Um," said Chris. He looked at Omar. Omar looked back.

Pamela walked closer to the jungle gym.

"We will help you look for land halfway up," called Chris. He climbed on the first rung of the jungle gym.

"Okay," said Bobby. "I am the top watchman, and you are the bottom watchmen. When you spot land, yell, 'Land ho!' "

"Okay," said Omar. He started to climb next to Chris.

"Why don't you all be top watchmen?" Pamela called to Chris.

Chris looked at her. "No, that is okay," he said. "I like being a bottom watchman."

"Me too," said Omar.

"You are afraid," said Pamela. She turned to Jannie and Leslie. "Chris and Omar are afraid to climb to the top of the jungle gym."

Chris frowned at Pamela. So did Omar.

"We do not need three top watchmen," said Omar.

Pamela laughed. "That is not the reason," she said. "The reason is you are afraid to go higher."

"Am not," said Chris.

"Are too," said Pamela. "If you are not afraid, then I *dare* you to climb higher. Go all the way to the top."

Sara, Ian, Natalie, and Hank had come closer to hear what was going on.

Chris looked at Bobby, who was at the top of the jungle gym. He looked down at the ground. "I am not afraid, but I do not feel like climbing to the top of the jungle gym."

"You are both big babies," said Pamela. "I could climb to the top of the jungle gym with one hand tied behind my back."

"Just be quiet, Pamela," Omar said angrily.

"Babies, babies," said Pamela in a singsong voice. "Chris and Omar are both babies. Scaredy-cats."

"Stop that!" said Chris. He looked very angry.

Pamela thought it was funny that Chris and Omar were scared to climb higher.

"Bye-bye, babies," said Pamela, wiggling her fingers. "See you in nursery school." She walked away, giggling. Jannie and Leslie walked with her. "They should just admit it," said Pamela. "It is silly to pretend not to be scared."

"Really silly," Jannie agreed.

"I'll say," said Leslie as they headed back to the classroom.

A SURPRISING
ANNOUNCEMENT

"Good morning, class," said Ms. Colman on Thursday.

"Good morning, Ms. Colman," said the kids in 2A.

Ms. Colman asked Nancy to take attendance. Nancy found that everyone was present.

"Thank you," said Ms. Colman. "Now, class, I have some exciting news. I have just learned about a new exhibit at the Bedford Zoo. It is an exhibit about baby animals. It will start next week."

"Oh, boy," said Natalie. "I will ask my

parents to take me there next weekend."

"Actually," said Ms. Colman, "I have planned for us to take a field trip to the Bedford Zoo. We will go there in two weeks."

"All right!" said Hank. He punched the air.

"Hooray!" said Karen, bouncing in her seat. "I love the zoo!"

"What animals will we see there?" asked Sara.

"Many different kinds," answered Ms. Colman. "You will be able to pet and even hold some of the babies. In the meantime, we will continue to learn about animal babies. Please open your science books to page sixty-six."

"Wow! I want to hold a baby animal!" whispered Leslie. "Maybe even a lion cub, or a baby deer, like Bambi."

Pamela just looked at Leslie. She pulled out her textbook and flipped to the correct page. On page sixty-six were several photographs. One picture was of a tiger cub. Its mouth was open, showing tiny, sharp little teeth. Another picture showed a mother snake, surrounded by dozens of slippery baby snakes. Just looking at that picture made Pamela shiver. There was also a picture of a nest of baby mice. They looked pink and squishy.

Pamela swallowed hard. All these baby animals looked scary, maybe even more scary than grown-up animals. Pamela had a secret: She did not like animals. Her family had never had pets, other than her father's aquarium of rare fish. And Pamela did not have to touch those. She did not even have to feed them.

She had never liked any of her friends' pets. Dogs were all yelpy and jumpy, and cats hissed and scratched. Other animals were yucky too. Horses could bite, and a cow could stomp on your foot and break it. A goat could butt you with its horns. That would hurt.

Going to the zoo was okay, because all the animals were in habitats. They could not get out. But this field trip sounded awful. Getting up close to mothers and babies? Touching or even holding a baby animal? Pamela would rather walk on a tightrope.

Maybe not everyone would have to touch an animal. Maybe Pamela could just watch others touch them. But she would still have to be pretty close to them. What if an animal broke free and jumped on her? What if one bit her?

Pamela felt almost sick just thinking about it. All of her classmates were still talking excitedly about the field trip. Each person had a favorite animal that he or she hoped to see. But Pamela knew this was going to be the worst field trip ever.

FIELD TRIPS ARE STUPID

For the next few days Pamela tried hard not to think about the field trip. It was two weeks away. Anything could happen. Maybe Ms. Colman would decide a field trip was too much trouble. Maybe no one's parents would volunteer to come along and help out. Maybe they would have a late-spring blizzard, with lots of feet of snow.

During school, though, everyone talked about baby animals all the time.

"Will you stop talking about that stupid field trip?" Pamela asked Jannie at lunch the following Tuesday.

24

Jannie looked surprised. "I cannot help it," she said. "I am so excited. What if there is a baby elephant?"

A baby elephant could sit on me and mash me flat as a pancake, Pamela thought. Her stomach began to hurt and she pushed her sandwich away.

"Yeah, or a baby sea lion," said Leslie excitedly.

"My brother heard that the zoo has a special place where you can even pet baby sharks," said Sara.

"Baby sharks!" cried Leslie. "I would be scared to pet one of those."

"Me too," said Jannie.

Me three, thought Pamela, but she did not say it.

Jannie looked at her. "I bet Pamela would pet a baby shark," she said proudly.

Pamela stared at her. Was Jannie teasing her? Did Jannie know she was afraid of animals?

"You are right," said Leslie. "Pamela is not scared of anything. She said she could climb the jungle gym with one hand tied behind her back."

That is different, Pamela thought. Being up high is not scary. Being mushed flat by an elephant is scary.

"No one would have to pet a baby shark if our field trip got canceled," said Pamela.

"Canceled?" said Sara. "Why would it be canceled?"

"It had better not be canceled," said Jannie. "I am dying to go. Aren't you?"

"Yes," said Leslie.

"No," said Pamela. She did not want anyone to find out that she was afraid of animals, even baby ones. "This field trip sounds stupid. Baby animals — who cares? Baby animals are for babies." She spoke loudly, and Tammy turned around from the next table. Pamela waited for Jannie and Leslie to agree with her.

"Why do you say that?" asked Jannie. "I love baby animals."

"They are stupid," said Pamela. "I

wish we would go on an *interesting* field trip."

"I think the zoo sounds very interesting," said Sara.

"I always like going to the zoo," said Tammy.

"I would rather go . . . shopping," said Pamela. It was the first thing she could think of. She looked at Jannie and Leslie. "Wouldn't you?"

"Um," said Jannie.

"Maybe it is a *little* babyish," said Leslie. "But I love seeing all the animals. One time when I was there with my mother, I saw the male lion roaring, roaring, roaring. It was so loud. It was great."

Just the idea of seeing a huge, fierce lion roaring was enough to make Pamela feel all shaky inside. But she did not dare show it.

"Well," she said, putting her nose in the air, "I still say this field trip sounds stupid."

"Um, I guess it is also fun to go shopping," said Leslie.

Pamela could tell that Jannie and Leslie did not agree with her. But at least they were not arguing with her. Pamela shrugged as if she did not care one way or another. She took a sip of milk but could not eat any more lunch. She was still too upset, thinking about the big lion roaring in her ear.

6

THE RUNAWAY DOG

After lunch Pamela, Jannie, and Leslie walked outside. Pamela did not feel like playing anything, not even foursquare. She just wanted to sit and think of a way to not go on the field trip.

She plopped down on a bench near the oak tree.

"Do you want to play hopscotch, or jump rope?" asked Jannie.

"Neither," said Pamela.

Jannie and Leslie looked at each other.

"What is wrong, Pamela?" asked Leslie.

"Nothing," Pamela said grumpily.

There was a gate in the playground

fence not far from Pamela's bench. It was supposed to be shut at all times, but right now it was open a little bit.

Ricky and Hank were playing catch nearby. Their baseball gloves were on. Hank was wearing his baseball cap. Back and forth, back and forth they threw the ball. Pamela could not think of anything more boring.

"Woof!"

Pamela jumped. She looked up to see a dog standing next to the fence. His owner was tugging gently on his leash.

"Come along, Rex," said the dog's owner. "Those boys cannot play fetch with you right now."

"Woof!" said Rex. He pulled against his leash, and the man pulled back.

"Hi, doggy," said Ricky through the fence. He held up his softball. "Do you like to play ball?"

"WOOF!" barked Rex loudly. He gave a sudden lunge, and pulled his leash free. Then he ran to the gate and pushed it open with his nose.

Pamela gasped. "A dog! A dog!" she cried. She leaped up.

The dog looked at her, his mouth open.

"It is a puppy," said Jannie. "He is a golden retriever puppy. My cousin had one. He is awfully pretty."

Rex stood still for a moment, looking around. His owner came through the school-yard gate to get him. Then, with his tail wagging and ears flopping, Rex bounded toward Pamela.

"Oh, no!" cried Pamela. She jumped off the bench. A dog! A horrible dog! He was going to bite her or jump on her or slobber on her! His paws were probably muddy, and he would get mud all over her coat! Pamela started to run across the playground. When she looked back, the dog was chasing her. He was catching up.

"Help!" yelled Pamela. "Help! Save me!"

Racing across the playground, Pamela saw the jungle gym. Dogs probably could not climb jungle gyms.

Pamela could barely hear Leslie call, "He is just a puppy, Pamela!"

Pamela ran to the jungle gym as fast as she could. When she reached it, she scrambled up the bottom rungs. The dog stopped below her and barked. Pamela almost lost her grip, but she kept climbing. Higher and higher, so the dog could not reach her. When she looked down, he was standing on his hind legs, his front paws on the bottom rung.

Was he trying to come after her?

Her heart pounding, Pamela climbed up and up. Finally she was at the very top of the jungle gym. She was breathing hard, and she was very hot under her coat. Her hat had fallen off somewhere, and her hair was messy. She had torn one of her tights while she was climbing the jungle gym.

Down at the bottom, the dog barked up at her, his tail wagging.

"Go away!" shouted Pamela. "Go away, you dumb dog!"

The dog cocked his ears and looked at Pamela.

Then Pamela saw that everyone on the playground was watching her. The dog's owner rushed to him and grabbed Rex's leash.

"Naughty Rex," he said firmly. Then he looked up at Pamela. "He will not hurt you. He is just a puppy. He was trying to be friendly."

Pamela glared at him. Trying to be friendly! Was he bananas?

Chris was standing next to the man. He grinned at Pamela, then petted the dog. "Nice puppy," Chris said cheerfully. "Good dog." The dog panted and wagged his tail.

Omar stepped forward. He petted the dog's head. "What a nice dog," he said. "He is so *gentle* and *friendly*."

"He would never hurt anyone," said Rex's owner. "I am sorry you were scared," he called to Pamela.

Scared! Pamela started to deny it. Then she realized that everyone in the whole yard had seen her run away from the dog. They had seen her yell for help. They had seen her climb the jungle gym. And here she was, still at the very top.

"Come on down, Pamela," called Chris. "Come pet the nice puppy."

Pamela thought about climbing down. After all, the dog had not bitten anyone yet. But then Rex barked. Pamela stayed where she was.

"I am sorry," said the man again. He told everyone good-bye, then led Rex out of the playground. He latched the gate firmly behind him.

"Pamela is afraid of dogs," said Chris. "What else are you afraid of?"

"Pamela never feeds Hootie," said Ricky. "She never takes him home on week-ends."

"She is afraid of him too," said Omar. "Afraid of a little puppy. Afraid of a guinea pig."

Omar and Chris started laughing. They slapped high fives.

"That is why you do not want to go on the field trip," said Sara. "You do not like even tiny baby animals."

Pamela wanted to disappear. Jannie and Leslie looked up at her. Pamela started to climb down slowly. Her secret was out.

7
AWFUL ART

Pamela did not want to go to school the next day. She knew the kids would tease her. But it turned out not to be so bad. Once Chris sneaked up behind her and barked, making her jump. And Natalie mentioned that she had a very nice dog at home. A dog who did not mind if Natalie's socks fell down. Pamela's cheeks burned.

Other than that, no one teased her very much. Of course, Karen pointed out that she had two dogs and two cats, because she had two houses. (Karen's parents were divorced. Mostly Karen lived with her mother. But she spent every other weekend at her father's house.)

Pamela made it through the week.

After lunch on Friday, Ms. Colman handed a sheet of paper to each student. On each sheet was a drawing of some kind of animal. Some of them were mammals. Some were reptiles. Some were birds. The pictures were not colored in.

There were three baskets of art supplies on a desk. One basket held scraps of fake fur. One basket was full of feathers in all colors and sizes. The last basket held strips of vinyl printed to look like different kinds of reptile skin.

"You may color your animal any way you want," said Ms. Colman. "Then you may add fur or feathers or skin, depending on your animal."

Pamela's animal was a turtle. She took out her crayons and colored its head and legs green. She gave it brown eyes.

Chris leaned over her shoulder. "Is that a barking turtle?" he asked.

Pamela scowled at him.

"Maybe it is a snapping turtle," said

38

Omar. "Snap! Snap!" He clapped his hands together as if they were a turtle's mouth.

Pamela pretended she did not hear him. She left her desk and went to the front of the room. In the reptile basket she found some thin pieces of plastic that were stiff like a turtle's shell. She brought them back to her desk.

Next to her, Leslie was gluing pieces of fake fur onto her picture of a bat. Pamela could hardly stand to look at the picture.

She thought bats were disgusting and probably mean.

Leslie glanced over at Pamela. "That is a nice picture of a turtle," she said.

"Thank you," said Pamela. Leslie and Jannie had not teased her once about the dog. They had not even mentioned it. Pamela was glad they were her friends. "Turtles are probably slimy."

Leslie looked surprised. "No," she said. "Sometimes they are wet, if they have been swimming. But they are not slimy. A friend of my brother's had a turtle. He let me pet it. The shell was hard and smooth. Like Tupperware."

"Oh," said Pamela. She had never touched a turtle. She did not want to.

"Leslie, that is a very nice bat," said Ms. Colman.

"Thank you," said Leslie. "I like bats."

You *like* bats? Pamela thought in horror. Are you bananas? Pamela almost said that out loud. But she did not want to tease Leslie, since Leslie had not teased her.

"Bats are very interesting creatures," said Ms. Colman. "There might be some baby bats at the zoo exhibit."

"Cool," said Leslie.

Pamela felt sick.

"When you are done with your pictures," said Ms. Colman, "you may hang them on the bulletin board. Then we will play a guessing game about animals."

For the guessing game, Ms. Colman gave each student an index card. The index card had three clues about an animal on it. The kids were supposed to read the clues aloud, then guess what animal they were about.

Karen went first. (She always tried to be first, Pamela thought.)

"I am cream-colored with big brown spots," she read.

"A jaguar!" shouted Ricky. Karen shook her head.

"I live on the African savanna," said Karen.

"A leopard!" cried Bobby.

41

"I am very, very tall," said Karen.

"A giraffe?" guessed Natalie.

"Yes!" said Karen.

Big deal, thought Pamela. Anyone could have guessed that. She was glad the bell rang before it was time for her to read her index card. The week was over. One more week until the field trip.

LIBRARY PROJECT

"Good morning, class," said Ms. Colman on Monday. "This week we will have a special library project. It will help us get ready for our field trip next week."

Pamela almost groaned out loud.

"It will be your job to choose an animal — any kind of animal — and find books in the library that tell you about it," said Ms. Colman. "Try to find out about your animal's babies. For example, are they born live or do they hatch from eggs? How do their mothers care for them? What do they eat?"

Tammy raised her hand. "I already know what animal I want to learn about," she said. "I choose kangaroos."

"That is a good idea," said Ms. Colman. "After you learn about your animal, you will write a report on it. Your report should be at least ten sentences long. It will be due on Friday. And our field trip is next Tuesday."

"Yea!" said Audrey.

Yuck, thought Pamela.

"I do not know what animal to choose," Pamela told Ms. Colman. Class 2A was in the library. Most people had already chosen their animals and were looking for books about them.

"Well, what is your favorite animal?" asked Ms. Colman.

"I do not have one," said Pamela truthfully.

"Hmm," said Ms. Colman. "Your picture of a turtle was very nice. Would you like to learn more about turtles?"

Pamela thought about it. She did not really want to learn about turtles. But she did not have much choice. And maybe turtles would not be so bad. Any animal that felt like Tupperware could not be totally horrible.

"Okay," said Pamela.

Ms. Colman and Mr. Counts, the librarian, helped Pamela find books on turtles in the nonfiction section. Pamela sat down on the floor and looked through several of them. She was surprised to find that there were many, many kinds of turtles. Some were very small. One kind was so large that a child could ride on its back. Some lived only on land. Some lived both in water and on land. And some lived almost all the time in water. These were called sea turtles.

Sea turtles were kind of pretty. They were pale green. They lived in the ocean. Pamela did not think she would run into one anytime soon. She decided to write about sea turtles.

"Snap, snap!" said Omar, clapping his hands by Pamela's head. She jumped, then glared at him.

"Will you stop that?" she whispered.

"What is the matter, Pamela?" said Omar. "Did you think I was a fierce, man-eating puppy?"

Pamela narrowed her eyes. "I guess there is only one way to get away from you," she whispered. "I will have to climb to the top of the jungle gym."

Omar quit grinning. He frowned at her. "At least I am not scared of puppies and guinea pigs," he whispered back. Then

he turned and went to another part of the library.

Pamela looked down at her book. If someone had not left the playground gate open, no one would have found out her secret. Then Pamela would not be teased all the time. She hated being teased.

She read some more about turtles. Dumb old turtles. She picked up two books and took them to Mr. Counts to check out.

9

SEA TURTLES

The leatherback sea turtle can grow to be longer than six feet and weigh more than seven hundred pounds.

Gee, Pamela thought. That is one humongous turtle.

Ms. Colman's class was working on their reports. Pamela was reading a book called *Into the Sea*, which was all about sea turtles. She also had an article from a *National Geographic* magazine. Pamela's father had helped her read it at home.

"Wow!" said Ricky. "Did you know that a wild lion can practically eat its weight in raw meat? All at one time."

"Listen to this," said Hannie. "Beavers'

front teeth grow their whole life. If they did not always gnaw on trees, their teeth would grow so long that they could hurt themselves."

Pamela tried to shut her ears. She hated hearing all these weird facts about animals. The more she knew about them, the scarier they seemed. This project was making her miserable.

Pamela had already started to write her report. It was not due until Friday, but the sooner she wrote it, the sooner she could forget about sea turtles. She did not think sea turtles were as bad as lions or beavers. But she was ready for the baby-animal unit to be over.

Sea Turtles
by Pamela Harding

There are eight different kinds of sea turtles. All of them might become extinct. The smallest sea turtle is the olive ridley. It is two and a half feet long when it is grown up. The biggest one is the leatherback. It can be six feet long. It can weigh seven hundred pounds.

Sea turtles live almost all the time in the ocean. But they need air to breathe. That is because they are reptiles. They are not fish.

Sea turtles come on land to lay their eggs. Their eggs are the size of Ping-Pong balls. Sometimes people steal turtle eggs and eat them. Yuck.

Scientists are trying to figure out how to save sea turtles. It would be sad if they were all gone. The end.

Pamela thought about writing "*very* sad" if turtles were all gone, but decided not to. Just "sad" was okay. There. Her report was done.

"Pamela, guess what?" Leslie said. "Bats can eat more than twenty thousand insects a night."

"Oh, yuck," said Pamela. She wrinkled her nose.

"Cool," said Bobby. "Do they have insect-breath in the morning?"

Leslie giggled.

Pamela felt queasy. "Just be quiet, Bobby," she ordered. "Do not be such a baby. Only babies make jokes like that."

Bobby looked a little angry. Then he smiled a mean smile. "You are wrong, Pamela," he said. "Only babies are afraid of puppies. So what does that make you?"

"I am not a baby," said Pamela.

"Oh, yeah?" said Chris. "Only babies are afraid of guinea pigs. Wah, wah."

"I am not afraid of Hootie. I just think he stinks," said Pamela.

"You are scared to go on our field trip," said Omar. "You are probably going to be scared of the tiny baby animals."

"Will not!" said Pamela.

"She will probably stay home sick on Tuesday," said Bobby. "She will be too scared to even come."

"I will not!" said Pamela. She could not admit that she had thought about pretending to be sick that day.

"I dare you to come on the field trip," Chris taunted her.

"I dare you to pet a baby animal — any one," said Omar.

"That is not good enough. I dare you to pick up and *hold* a baby animal," said Bobby. He laughed. "I know you will not do it."

Pamela stood up and put her hands on her hips. "No problem," she insisted. "I will show you. You are the babies, not me."

The boys laughed. "We will see," said Chris.

Oh, no. What have I done now? thought Pamela.

10

PAMELA'S PROBLEM

"Mom!" called Tamara. "Have you seen my new jeans?"

Pamela's sixteen-year-old sister ran down the stairs. Pamela was sitting at the kitchen table, doing her homework. She was trying hard not to think about the field trip the next day. All last week Chris, Omar, and Bobby had reminded Pamela about their dare. They said if she did not hold a baby animal, they would write "Pamela Is the Biggest Baby at Stoneybrook Academy" on T-shirts. Then they would wear the T-shirts every day for a month.

"Which new jeans?" asked Pamela.

"The ones with the daisies on them," said Tamara.

"I saw Daddy put them in the laundry basket," said Pamela.

Tamara smiled at her. "Thanks."

Pamela watched her sister fish the jeans out of the piles of clean laundry. Tamara was the best big sister ever. She never teased Pamela or made her feel like a baby. She let Pamela borrow her perfume sometimes. She let Pamela try her fingernail polish and her makeup. She even let Pamela stay in the room when her friends from high school came over. It made Pamela feel very cool. Pamela wished she could be friends with Tamara's friends all the time. But she could not. Mostly she had to be friends with other second-graders. And they mostly seemed like babies.

Pamela bet that Tamara's friends would not have dared her to hold a baby animal on the field trip.

Mrs. Harding was in her home office.

Pamela could hear her typing on her computer. Mr. Harding was asleep on his recliner in the den. He did that every night after dinner.

"Tam?" said Pamela. "I have a problem."

Tamara glanced up from the laundry. "Yeah? Like what?"

"It is a major problem," said Pamela.

"Oh. We better have an ice-cream sandwich, then." Tamara got two ice-cream sandwiches out of the freezer. She handed one to Pamela. "I have ten minutes before Maribeth gets here, so let's make this fast."

"Okay," said Pamela. She told Tamara the whole story, about the dog on the playground, and how Chris and Omar had been teasing her. She told Tamara about the dare on the field trip.

"Hmm. Well, I do not like animals that much either," admitted Tamara. "Except I think Daddy's fish are pretty."

Pamela nodded. She felt better knowing that Tamara, who was so cool, did not like animals.

"But I think you are going to have to hold one," Tamara went on. "Try to find a small one, then just hold it for a second. I think that is the only thing you can do."

"I will be too afraid," wailed Pamela.

"Try not to think about it," advised Tamara. "Pretend it is an ice-cream sandwich."

"What?" asked Pamela.

"Just look at the baby animal and pretend it is an ice-cream sandwich," said Tamara. "Then pick it up, like you pick up an ice-cream sandwich. Hold it for a second, then put it down. Boom. Problem solved."

Pamela looked at the last bit of her ice-cream sandwich. She tried to imagine it was a small, wiggling baby animal with fur or scales or feathers. It was hard. A small, wiggling baby animal would not be dripping vanilla ice cream on the kitchen table.

She looked at Tamara.

They both started laughing at the same time.

THE NIGHTMARE BEGINS

The next morning was the day of the field trip. Mrs. Harding drove Pamela to school. She gave Pamela three dollars to spend any way she wanted.

"Good-bye, honey," she said as they pulled up to Stoneybrook Academy. "Have a good time today." She gave Pamela a big smile.

Pamela did not want to get out of the car. She thought about saying she suddenly had a stomachache. But she could not. For one thing, it would be a fib. Her stomach felt fluttery, but she was not really sick. For another thing, Chris and Omar and Bobby and probably a bunch of other people in her class would know she had chickened out. The teasing would never stop.

For just a moment Pamela wished she had never teased Chris and Omar that day on the playground. Then maybe none of this would have happened. But she had thought they deserved it at the time. Second-graders should not be afraid to go to the top of the jungle gym.

"Mom?" she said. "Why don't we have a dog or a cat?"

"What?" asked Mrs. Harding. "Why do you ask?"

"I have been wondering."

"Well, when I was little, I had a cat. Her name was Silver. I loved her so much. She was the best cat in the whole world."

"Really?" Pamela had never heard this story.

"Yup. Then one summer we moved, and we could not take Silver with us. My grandmother kept her for us. Silver was very happy with her. And whenever we went to see Grammy, I could see Silver again. But it was not the same. And I felt so sad about it that I decided I did not want to have another cat again."

"Gee." This was amazing.

"But you know what?" said Mrs. Harding. "Maybe I would feel better about it now. Maybe it is time for me to think about getting another cat."

"Would the cat be mean?" asked Pamela.

"Oh, no," said Mrs. Harding. "Cats are usually not mean, unless you are mean to them. Silver was the sweetest cat in the whole world. Now, you better run on, honey. The bell is about to ring."

Pamela could see the kids in Ms. Colman's class on the playground. She did not have to rush inside. "What about dogs?" she asked.

"Oh, I do not like dogs very much," said Mrs. Harding. "They are all yappy and bouncy and muddy. They wet on the floor and chew your shoes. I would not like to have a dog."

Pamela smiled. She knew that other people thought dogs were wonderful. It cheered her up to know that her mother did not.

" 'Bye, Mom," she said. She kissed her mother and got out of the car.

"Okay, boys and girls," called Ms. Colman. "Please line up with your partners."

It was time for the field trip. Pamela and Leslie were partners. Jannie was partners with Tammy. Everyone in class 2A lined up, ready to get on the big yellow school bus that would take them to the zoo. Behind Jannie and Tammy were Audrey and Sara, Hannie and Nancy, Karen and Terri, Chris and Omar (of course), Ian and Hank, Bobby and Ricky, and Natalie and Ms. Colman.

"Does everyone have his or her lunch?" asked Ms. Colman.

"Yes!" the whole class said.

"Okay, then. Start filing onto the bus. Remember your manners."

Pamela and Leslie sat on the long seat at the very back of the bus. Jannie and Tammy sat next to them. To Pamela's dismay, Chris and Omar sat right in front of her.

"Remember our dare," said Chris. "I am surprised you came today. I thought you would pretend to be sick."

Pamela stuck her nose in the air. "You are wrong. I am not afraid of baby animals. I will have no problem touching one."

"You have to *hold* one," Omar pointed out. "Pick one up."

"Fine." Pamela tried to look calm, but inside she felt as if she were in the middle of an earthquake. She did not know if she could hold one. But she knew she had to, somehow.

12

ZOO TOUR

It took almost an hour to drive to Bedford, where the zoo was. The bus ride was boring, boring, boring. Some kids were singing dumb songs like "The Wheels on the Bus" and "A Hundred Bottles of Pop." Pamela wished they would be quiet.

Instead of singing, Pamela, Leslie, Jannie, and Tammy talked. Tammy had brought her latest *Cricket* magazine, and they took turns reading it.

"I cannot wait to get to the zoo," said Leslie.

"It is better than a whole day of school," said Jannie.

"Yes," said Pamela. "But I wish we

were going to Adventure World instead."

"That would be so fun," said Leslie.

"I love Adventure World," said Jannie.

"Okay, class, here we are," called Ms. Colman from the front of the bus.

Everyone cheered. Pamela did not.

"Remember, we will be in two groups," said Ms. Colman. "I will lead one group, and our room father, Mr. Ford, will lead the other. First we will tour the zoo. Then we will have a picnic lunch. Then we will see the special baby-animal exhibit."

Chris leaned over and made a spooky sound at Pamela. "Oooh-oooh," he said softly. "Not baby animals!" He opened his eyes wide. "Baby animals! Oh no! Save me! Saaave meeeee!" He pretended to fall down in his seat, kicking and thrashing.

Omar was laughing so hard that he almost fell over too.

Pamela set her jaw and stared out the window.

"Is there a problem back there?" said Ms. Colman.

Chris popped up into place. "No."

"Good. Everyone off the bus."

The zoo was a good place for animals, Pamela decided half an hour later. It was much better than animals out in nature. For one thing, Pamela knew the animals could not escape. For another thing, as soon as you got bored, you could move on to another habitat.

Pamela and Leslie were in Mr. Ford's group. Thankfully, Chris and Omar were in Ms. Colman's group. Pamela tried to relax and prepare herself to hold a baby animal. She tried to look as if she saw wild animals every day and they did not bother her.

"Wow! Look at those huge teeth!" Audrey said when they saw the hippo yawn.

"Hmm, yes," Pamela said in a bored tone.

"That cheetah is running so fast," said Bobby a little while later. "I bet it could catch anything."

"Uh-huh," said Pamela. She looked down at her zoo map.

The Bedford Zoo was not as big as the Bronx Zoo in New York City or the National Zoo in Washington, D.C. But the habitats made the animals feel at home, and many spring flowers were in bloom. Pamela enjoyed looking at the tulips and daffodils and hyacinths.

That morning, Mr. Ford's group saw practically the whole zoo. Pamela liked the rhinos and zebras the best, because they were the farthest away. There was a large bird enclosure, which she hated. Birds flew overhead, squawking, and there was bird doo on the ground. Pamela was afraid that a bird would swoop down and bite her. She walked slowly and stiffly through the exhibit.

When it came time to go into the reptile house, Pamela held Leslie's hand a little bit tighter. Leslie squeezed her hand and smiled at her. Pamela smiled back tightly. Inside the reptile house it was dark and warm. The walls were lined with exhibits of snakes, lizards, and frogs.

"Frogs are amphibians," said Ricky.

Whoop-de-do, thought Pamela. Then she saw an exhibit of turtles. They were behind glass, with a small pool to swim in and rocks to climb on. They were walking slowly around their habitat. Their sign said SNAPPING TURTLES.

"Chomp, chomp," said Bobby, coming up behind Pamela. "I bet that turtle could take your finger right off."

Pamela felt like crying. Bobby had ruined even turtles for her. The rest of the time she was in the reptile house, Pamela kept her eyes on the pictures and fact cards on the opposite wall.

Ms. Colman's group was waiting for them outside. "Time for lunch," Ms. Colman said cheerfully.

13

THE BABY-ANIMAL EXHIBIT

Ms. Colman's class ate lunch on picnic tables near the Education Center. The sun shone down warmly, and there was no breeze. Mrs. Harding had packed a special lunch for Pamela of hot-and-sour soup, a Chinese spring roll, and almond cookies for dessert.

Chris ate his peanut-butter sandwich as if he were a tiger devouring a gazelle. "Rrhhhhgh," he growled, shaking his head from side to side. Crumbs flew out of his mouth. Pamela looked at him calmly, wishing he had come down with chicken pox today.

"Okay, everyone," said Ms. Colman. "When you are finished, please throw away your trash. Then line up over here with your partners. It is time for the baby-animal exhibit."

Suddenly Pamela's almond cookie tasted like sand in her mouth. She swallowed hard and took a sip of milk. This was what she had been dreading for two weeks.

The baby-animal exhibit was divided into several different areas. Outside in small corrals were baby goats, lambs, and pigs. There were also a miniature donkey and some calves. In large cages around the corral were bunnies, ducks, and other animals. In a building next door were babies who could not be outside yet.

"Hello!" said a woman. Her name tag said SHERRY MCDONALD, ZOOKEEPER. "You must be Ms. Colman's class."

"Yes, that's us," said Ms. Colman.

"Come on in," said Ms. McDonald.

She held open the gate that led to the small corral. Inside the ground was hard, packed dirt. Lambs and baby goats saw them enter and ran to them.

Ms. McDonald laughed. "They think you will give them a treat," she explained. "Here." She handed out small pieces of chow that looked like dog kibbles. Sara, Karen, Hannie, and Jannie got some, and so did all the boys. The baby goats and lambs eagerly nibbled the chow, right out of their hands.

Hannie laughed. "This tickles," she said. "Her tongue is so soft."

Pamela shivered. The thought of a baby goat nibbling at her hand made her feel panicky.

A lamb started nosing around Leslie, and Leslie patted her. Pamela tried to back away casually, so no one would notice.

"This is a hedgehog," said Ms. McDonald. She opened a hutch and pulled out a small brown pincushion. "His name is Moses. He's very shy. That's why he is all

huddled up. You may touch him gently on his back. Use just two fingers."

Ricky, Chris, and Natalie stepped forward and stroked the hedgehog gently.

"He is so prickly," said Natalie. "Can he hurt us with his quills?"

"Well," said Ms. McDonald, "it is a myth that hedgehogs or porcupines can shoot their quills at an enemy. But a porcupine can let go of its quills, so that they stick into an attacker."

Great, thought Pamela. She edged away from the hedgehog. She was feeling very unhappy. This trip was horrible. If she had come with her parents, she could just walk around and enjoy herself. Now she felt as if everyone in her class were watching whatever she did. And she knew it was just a matter of time before Chris and Omar remembered their dare. What was she going to do?

She had not seen one animal yet that she thought she could pick up. She wished she were at home.

"Hey, look," said Audrey. "Next door

they have baby reptiles and birds. There are a baby iguana and a baby snake. There is even a baby ostrich. Let's go look at them."

"Is that what you will pick up?" asked Chris. He was standing in front of Pamela. "Will you pick up a baby snake?"

Pamela lifted her chin higher in the air. "You did not say it had to be a snake," she said.

"No," said Chris. "But you have to pick up something. I dare you."

The other kids in Ms. Colman's class were quiet. Leslie squeezed Pamela's hand again, as if to tell her she did not need to do it. But Pamela knew she did. The rest of second grade would be terrible if she did not pick up a baby animal.

"Okay," she said. "But I have to go to the bathroom first."

Pamela turned and walked out of the baby-animal exhibit. She went through the gate and broke into a run.

HARRIET AND THE TORTOISES

No one was allowed to leave the exhibit without telling Ms. Colman or Mr. Ford. But that is what Pamela did. She did not care if she got into trouble. She did not care about anything except getting away from all the animals.

Her eyes filled with tears. Suddenly, *wham!* She ran into something and fell backward.

"Are you okay?" asked a woman's voice. Strong hands picked Pamela up and set her on her feet.

Pamela was crying now, trying to cover her face.

"Are you hurt?" asked the woman.

Pamela shook her head.

"Listen, my name is Harriet," said the woman. "I am a zookeeper here. Are you lost? Please tell me what is wrong."

Pamela looked up. The woman was wearing a zoo uniform. Her name tag said HARRIET SISKO. Pamela found herself blurting out the whole story about Chris and Omar and their dare, and how afraid she was of animals, and how all the animals she had seen were yucky.

"Now I have to hold one!" she wailed. "But I cannot. And if I do not, Chris and Omar will tease me for the rest of second grade. I will have to change schools."

"Hmm." Harriet scratched her chin. "It is too bad Chris and Omar are picking on you. It is not nice to tease someone about something they are scared of."

Pamela bit her lip and looked at the ground. She had teased Chris and Omar about being scared of the jungle gym. This whole thing was almost her own fault.

"I'll tell you what, Pamela," said Harriet. "Come with me into a special part of the exhibit. I want to show you something."

They were standing in front of a brick building that said ZOO NURSERY on it.

"This is where we keep animals that are too small for the exhibit," Harriet said. "Usually babies stay with their mothers for about seven weeks. Sometimes the mother cannot care for them. Then we feed them and make sure they are all right."

ZOO
NURSERY

Inside the zoo nursery were several different rooms. The nursery looked almost like a hospital. Zoo workers bustled around. One woman held a baby bear wrapped in a towel. She was feeding him with a bottle. He held it in his paws like a human baby.

"This is Buster," said Harriet. "He is about nine weeks old."

"Oh," said Pamela. Buster already had long claws.

"We will try to find some animal baby that you can hold," Harriet told Pamela. "Let's look in here." She pushed a door open and they went into another room. The walls were lined with large steel cages.

"Here is a baby duck," said Harriet. "It is about three weeks old. Would you like to try holding it?"

Pamela looked at the baby duck. It did not have feathers yet. It was covered with soft yellow down. It had small orange feet and a small orange beak. Its eyes were shiny and black.

"No, thank you," said Pamela.

"How about this bunny?" asked Harriet. She opened a cage and brought out a tiny bunny. Its ears were not very long yet. It looked sleepy and soft.

"Does it have teeth?" asked Pamela.

"Small ones," said Harriet. She showed her. "Here, stroke its fur right behind the ears."

Pamela reached out and gently touched the bunny. The bunny opened its eyes and looked at her. Pamela pulled her hand back.

"This bunny is just like a human baby in some ways," said Harriet. "He still drinks his mother's milk. He still sleeps a lot. He still needs protection."

Protection? Pamela had not thought of that before. She had thought that just about any animal was dangerous and could bite. She had not realized that small baby animals — and maybe even some big animals — needed to be protected themselves.

"Would you like to hold this bunny?"

asked Harriet. "And show your friends?"

Pamela wanted to say yes. But the bunny was kind of . . . wiggly. She was afraid she would drop it. "I do not think so," she whispered.

Close by was a terrarium. It had sand and rocks at the bottom.

"What is in there?" asked Pamela.

"Those are star tortoises," said Harriet. "They are not actually babies. They are about two years old. We are giving these little guys some vitamins and medicine to build up their strength."

Inside the terrarium were several turtles the size of Pamela's hand. They had little legs and little faces. Their shells were dark brown, with small yellow starbursts all over them. They were very, very pretty.

Pamela looked at Harriet and smiled.

15

TURTLE VICTORY

"It is a star tortoise," said Pamela confidently. Harriet had let her carry one of the tortoises out to the petting yard. Now everyone in Ms. Colman's class, including Chris and Omar, were gathered around her.

"It is from India," Pamela continued. "It is called a star tortoise because of the markings on its shell."

She held the tortoise carefully, like an ice-cream sandwich, and stroked its shell gently. "Isn't it pretty?"

"I never knew a tortoise could be so pretty," said Leslie.

"It is the prettiest tortoise I have ever seen," said Jannie.

Pamela smiled at them.

"Does it bite?" asked Chris hopefully.

"Nope," said Pamela. "It does not have teeth."

"What is the difference between a turtle and a tortoise?" asked Omar.

"Turtles usually swim a lot, and like water," explained Pamela. "Tortoises live on land."

Chris and Omar looked at Pamela. Pamela looked back at them. Then Chris nodded and Omar shrugged. They walked away.

Pamela felt like singing.

Soon it was time to get back on the school bus that would take Ms. Colman's class back to Stoneybrook. Pamela returned the star tortoise to Harriet and thanked her. Harriet had saved the day. Now Pamela would not have to change schools or be a second-grade dropout.

85

Once again a line of partners waited to get on the bus.

"Just a second, Leslie," said Pamela. "I have to talk to Chris and Omar."

Chris and Omar were at the back of the line. Pamela motioned them over to her.

"What do you want?" asked Omar suspiciously.

Pamela took a deep breath. "I want to apologize," she said. "I know it was mean to tease you about the jungle gym. People cannot help it if they are scared of something. I am sorry I made you feel bad."

Chris and Omar looked at each other.

"Well, that is okay, I guess," said Chris. "We got to tease you back. Now we are even."

"Yes, we are even," said Pamela. "And I will try not to tease you anymore."

"Us too," said Omar.

"Okay." Pamela and Chris and Omar shook hands.

When Pamela got back in line next to

Leslie, Leslie smiled at her. "I am proud of you," said Leslie.

"For holding a tortoise?" said Pamela.

"That, and for other things too," said Leslie. And she squeezed Pamela's hand.

L. GODWIN

About the Author

ANN M. MARTIN lives in New York and loves animals, especially cats. She has two cats of her own, Gussie and Woody.

Other books by Ann M. Martin that you might enjoy are *Rachel Parker, Kindergarten Show-Off* and the Baby-sitters Club series. She has also written the Baby-sitters Little Sister series starring Karen Brewer, one of the kids in Ms. Colman's class.

Ann grew up in Princeton, New Jersey, where she had many wonderful teachers like Ms. Colman. Ann likes ice cream, *I Love Lucy*, and especially sewing.